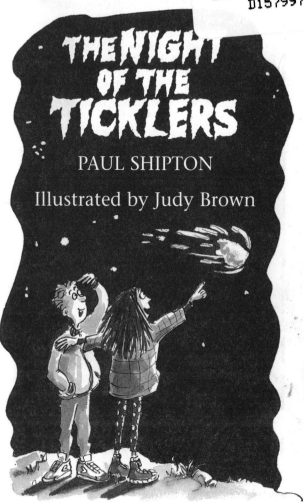

THE NIGHT OF THE TICKLERS

PAUL SHIPTON

Illustrated by Judy Brown

OXFORD
UNIVERSITY PRESS

04162

OXFORD
UNIVERSITY PRESS

Great Clarendon Street, Oxford OX2 6DP

Oxford University Press is a department of the University of Oxford.
It furthers the University's objective of excellence in research, scholarship,
and education by publishing worldwide in

Oxford   New York
Auckland   Cape Town   Dar es Salaam   Hong Kong   Karachi
Kuala Lumpur   Madrid   Melbourne   Mexico City   Nairobi
New Delhi   Shanghai   Taipei   Toronto

With offices in
Argentina   Austria   Brazil   Chile   Czech Republic   France   Greece
Guatemala   Hungary   Italy   Japan   Poland   Portugal   Singapore
South Korea   Switzerland   Thailand   Turkey   Ukraine   Vietnam

Oxford is a registered trade mark of Oxford University Press
in the UK and in certain other countries

First published 1996
This edition 2005

British Library Cataloguing in Publication Data
Data available

ISBN-13: 978-0-19-918412-5
ISBN-10: 0-19-918412-7

5 7 9 10 8 6 4

Available in packs
Stage 14 Pack of 6:
ISBN-13: 978-0-19-918406-4; ISBN-10: 0-19-918406-2
Stage 14 Class Pack:
ISBN-13: 978-0-19-918413-2; ISBN-10: 0-19-918413-5
Guided Reading Cards also available:
ISBN-13: 978-0-19-918415-6; ISBN-10: 0-19-918415-1

Cover artwork by Judy Brown

Printed in Great Britain by
Ashford Colour Press, Gosport Hants

CHAPTER 1

A bad start

The day got off to a bad start. Stoneface Watkins was in the middle of his most boring assembly ever (which is really saying something).

That's when Katy Skinner leaned forward and whispered to me, 'ZZZZZZZZZZZ! Boring! If there was a contest to find the most boring person, old Stoneface would be world champion. Wake me up when it's over!'

3

It wasn't all that funny, but I just couldn't help myself. I burst out laughing. (I always laugh at Katy's rotten jokes.) It came out in a long hiss, like gas coming out of a burst pipe. The more I tried to stop, the harder I laughed. That made Katy laugh too.

And that's when Stoneface Watkins' steel-grey eye fell on us. Of course, 'Stoneface' isn't his real name, but it suits him all right. Our Headteacher is the strictest, most miserable person on the planet. And there's one thing he hates above all other things... kids giggling during assembly.

His voice echoed around the hall like thunder.

'Katy Skinner! Mike Edwards! See me in my office after school!'

That's when I stopped laughing. And *that's* how the day got off to a bad start. I didn't know it then but my troubles hadn't even started yet...

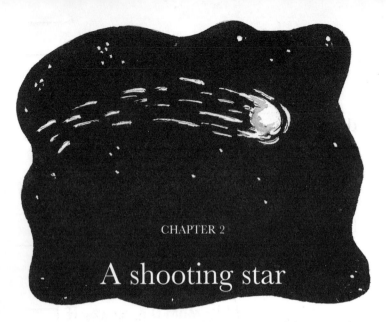

CHAPTER 2

A shooting star

Mr Watkins gave us the same old speech in his office that afternoon.

'You'll have to pull your socks up, I'm afraid, and learn that life is not one big joke. There are some things that you have to take seriously, and school is one of them. School is no laughing matter. And another thing...'

And so on.

6

We had heard it all before, but that didn't stop Stoneface Watkins from telling us again… and again.

When Katy and I finally left school, it was already dark. Our bikes looked lonely in the bike sheds. They were the last ones there.

Look at the time! My mum'll go crazy if I'm late for dinner.

She unchained her bike and gave me one of her cross looks.

This is all your fault, Mike Edwards! Why did you have to giggle like that in assembly?

7

MY fault? It was you who made me laugh...

But then Katy shrugged and flashed me her best grin, and I knew I couldn't stay angry with her. I never can. We began to cycle home.

'We can take the short cut by Overton's farm,' said Katy. 'That'll save us a few minutes...'

She turned off onto the jet-black path that snaked up through the woods and over the hill by Overton's farm. I followed. We had cycled halfway up the path when Katy let out a sudden shout.

'Stop!' Her brakes squealed.

I stopped alongside her.

Look! A shooting star!

Mm, yes, right.

Katy was always trying tricks like that, but I wasn't going to fall for it this time.

No, really. LOOK!

She pointed upwards, and I saw a single shooting star zip across the sky over the village of Puddlesford. At first it was just a point of light, like a diamond moving against the blackness.

I tried to sound as scientific as I could.

'"Shooting stars" aren't really stars at all. They're meteors – chunks of rock which zoom through space. They burn up if they enter the earth's atmosphere.'

Well, I've got news for you, professor... This one isn't burning up. It's going to land!

It was true! The point of light was getting bigger. We could see a long tongue of flame behind it now. It was coming closer, and getting brighter and brighter. I tried to tell Katy how unusual this was, but she couldn't hear my voice over the terrible din.

The meteor whooshed overhead and just missed the tops of the trees to our left. Then there was a dreadful crashing sound...

'What was that?' I whispered. My ears were ringing, but I could still hear my heart pounding.

Katy gave an excited grin. 'I don't know... but whatever it was, it just landed.'

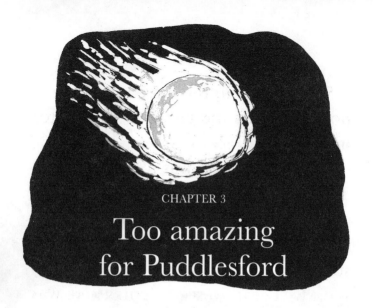

CHAPTER 3

Too amazing for Puddlesford

I could hardly believe what I'd just seen.

We'd better go and tell someone. The police or the fire brigade. Anyone!

Of course, Katy had other ideas.

She said, 'Are you nuts? This is the most amazing thing that has ever happened in Puddlesford, and we're going to be the first to see it. Come on!'

12

She rode off in the direction of the noise. I sighed and began to pedal after her.

Soon the ground was too bumpy to cycle on. We left our bikes and made our way through the trees on foot. I could feel my legs trembling with each step. At first it was totally dark, but soon we began to see a light. There was a faint purple glow ahead of us.

On the other side of the trees, we saw where the light was coming from. It was a huge hole in the ground.

Katy edged closer. I gulped and forced my legs to go on. We reached the edge of the crater and looked over. What we saw made our mouths drop open in surprise.

At the bottom of the hole there was a smooth, silver ball. It didn't look like any meteor I had ever heard of.

My mind raced. Was it...? Could it be...? My head was filled with thoughts of aliens and UFOs from all the science fiction stories I'd read.

The silver ball made a buzzing sound, and a door began to slide open in it. A door! I wanted to run, but I was frozen to the spot.

And then something began to come out of the ball...

CHAPTER 4

Aliens

It was the weirdest creature I'd ever seen.

In science fiction films there seem to be two kinds of aliens. Sometimes they're skinny little aliens with big heads, who are nice and friendly. And sometimes they're big, green scaly aliens who try to eat you, or melt your brain with a laser blaster.

16

But this one didn't look like either of those. To be honest, it looked rather funny. (Funny *ha ha*, that is.) Its chubby green body was round as a ball and it had two huge, wide feet. It had a stubby little nose, and a big, lop-sided grin. Its eyes twinkled with mischief.

But oddest of all were the creature's arms. They were long and bendy and each one ended in ten fingers. These fingers were long and slender, but they looked strong.

Katy and I watched in amazement as a second creature came out of the ball. It looked just like the first one. They didn't look scary at all – in fact, they looked friendly, in a goofy kind of way.

Katy cleared her throat. 'Hi there,' she said.

I couldn't believe it! This was probably the first meeting ever between a human being and an alien. Couldn't we think of something better to say than 'hi there'? This meeting would go down in the history books, after all.

The two creatures went on grinning, but they made no sound.

I raised one hand, and put on my best scientist-voice.

Greetings! We... er... the people of Planet Earth welcome you.

'You sound stupid!' hissed Katy. I took no notice.

So... um... where have you come from?

I pointed up at the stars to show that I was asking which planet they had come from. (Of course I knew they hadn't come from the next village!)

The two aliens looked slowly at each other, then they both let out a low sound.

Heh, heh, heh. Heh, heh, heh.

'I beg your pardon?' I said. (I was still trying to be polite.)

The creatures still didn't answer, but something did happen. Something very strange. They began to wave and shake and wobble their arms. As they did this, their arms began to grow longer. Soon their arms were twice as long. Then the aliens began to reach out towards us. Their fingers were waggling.

I still wasn't scared though. The aliens looked so funny and smiley. Maybe they want to shake hands, I thought. I held my right hand out, ready.

But the alien did not take hold of my hand. Instead, it began to waggle its fingers even more.

Hmmm, I thought. Maybe this is how they say hello on their planet?

The two aliens let out their low chuckle again.

Heh, heh, heh.

And then it happened...

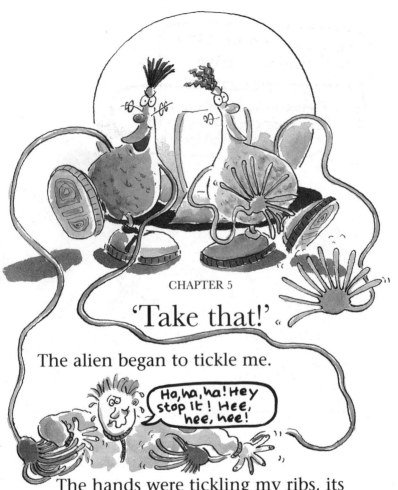

CHAPTER 5

'Take that!'

The alien began to tickle me.

Ha, ha, ha! Hey stop it! Hee, hee, hee!

The hands were tickling my ribs, its twenty fingers moving faster than the fastest typist. I could hear Katy giggling too. The other alien was tickling her.

22

Hoo, hoo, hoo, no, stop, stop, hahahahaha!

Aaaarrgh, heeheehee — no more — hahahaha hahahahaha!

I laughed and laughed until tears rolled down my cheeks, and my sides throbbed. I felt like I would explode. But still the alien tickled me. It was horrible! On and on I laughed.

Suddenly I heard Katy shout out.

Take that!

She smashed down on the alien's rubbery arms with both her fists. Katy always was the toughest kid in our village, and she proved it again now. The alien's grip was broken. It pulled its arms back in surprise.

24

Quick! Help meee-heeheeheeheehee!

Katy wasted no time. She rushed over and hammered down on the arms of the alien who was tickling me. The creature's grip loosened only for a split-second, but it was long enough. I jumped backwards out of its reach.

For a moment I wasn't sure what to do. The tickling had left me feeling dazed. But then Katy shouted, 'Run!'

So I did.

CHAPTER 6

Heh! heh! heh!

We charged back towards our bikes. I looked back over my shoulder. The aliens had climbed to the top of the crater and were waddling slowly forwards. They were waving their long, bendy arms and still making that same dark chuckle.

It didn't sound so friendly any more.

Heh, heh, heh.

For a few endless moments we couldn't find our bikes in the darkness. But then I bashed my shin on one of them.

Here!

We scrambled onto our bikes and began to pedal down the path to the village as fast as we could. My sides still ached from being tickled, but I didn't dare slow down.

'Where – where shall we go?' I gasped to Katy.

'Got to get help!' she panted back.

We swerved onto the road that led to the village.

As we raced along, my heart was thudding with fear and excitement. And yet there was a tiny part of me that couldn't help feeling disappointed. I had read lots of exciting science fiction books about aliens invading earth. They were always terrifying monsters that wanted to take over our planet. Proper enemies – not daft-looking creatures that tickled us until we gave up! It was embarrassing.

When we got to the village, the streets were quiet. Too quiet.

Shhhh! What's that?

I listened.

Aaaa - hahahahahahahahaha!

It was the sound of crazy laughter and it was coming from a house on our left. There was a Tickler in there! But they couldn't have beaten us down into the village, could they? It meant only one thing – there were more than two of them. But how many more?

29

The same sound was coming from the next house, and the next. The village of Puddlesford had already been invaded. We could hear Ticklers in every house! It seemed like the whole village was shaking with helpless laughter. A shiver ran down my spine.

Then someone stumbled out into the street in front of us. We had to swerve to miss him. It was Mr Marshall, the butcher. He was normally a jolly man, but I had never seen him like this before. A Tickler had fixed itself on to the butcher's big tummy, and Mr Marshall was letting out an awful, high-pitched giggle. His face – which was normally red – was now bright purple.

Katy and I jumped off our bikes and rushed to get the Tickler off the butcher. We each grabbed one of its arms and tugged with all our strength. No good!

Help meeee! Heeheeheehee heeheeheeheeheeheeheehee!

31

We began to bash down on its arms, but that didn't work either. Mr Marshall was helpless with laughter. The Tickler chuckled darkly and went on tickling.

It's impossible! They're getting stronger!

Suddenly we heard the noise from behind us.

Heh, heh, heh.

32

We spun around. Three more Ticklers were waddling down the street towards us. Another two came out from the shadows.

'Go!' I shouted, but Katy was already back on her bike and pedalling like crazy.

We zoomed down the street, leaving poor Mr Marshall behind us. We were faster than the Ticklers, but I knew we couldn't keep ahead of them forever.

We slowed down when we came to the corner of our road – the road where both our houses were. I could see dark shapes moving at the end of the street. The familiar pavements and front gardens echoed with the new sound of terrible laughter from within the houses.

My mind was filled with a picture of my Mum and Dad being tickled until they were as purple as Mr Marshall, and my brother Joel giggling crazily…

HEE AAAAA! HO HO HEE HEE HAA HAA! HEE!
HEE HEE! HEE! HAHA HAAAAA! HEE HEE!
HEE HEE! HEE! HAAAA HEE HEE! HOO HOO!
HEE HEE!

We've GOT to help them!

35

Katy shook her head, and I could see how big and afraid her eyes were.

No, there's too many Ticklers — we'd never make it...

The police! They'll know what to do!

I wasn't so sure. I mean, the Puddlesford police knew what to do if there was a robbery, or if someone parked their car on a double yellow line. But *this*? But I hadn't any other ideas to suggest, so we headed towards the police station on the High Street.

I passed a parked car and two ten-fingered hands made a grab for me. A Tickler! I just managed to dodge out of the way in time.

They're everywhere!

Don't worry, we're almost there, almost—

Katy's voice choked. I looked ahead and saw why. In the darkness we could see a crowd of small round shapes outside the police station. The Ticklers had surrounded it. We could hear the horrible chorus of their chuckles. There was another sound also – the laughter of the policemen and policewomen from inside. We would find no help there.

I glanced behind me. More Ticklers were waddling towards us. Panic seized me in its icy grip. It was clear what we had to do.

HOO HOO HEE HEE HEE HEE HEE HEE

POLICE

We've got to get out of Puddlesford. We've got to warn people!

Invasion

We started cycling out of the village. My legs ached, but I ignored the pain and forced them to go faster. It felt good to leave all the sound of laughter behind us. Now if we could just make it to the next village and get help...

40

'Look!' shouted Katy.

A car was parked in the middle of the road. Its lights were on and the driver's door was open. As we got closer we could hear a voice, but when we got there we realized it was coming from the radio. The car was empty.

And now the new smash hit number one song, 'Aren't I Cute?' from Boyz Club.

It was our local radio station. The song began and I was about to click the radio off when the DJ interrupted the music.

This is a news flash. Reports are coming in to the station from people who claim to have seen UFOs – Unidentified Flying Objects. Details are not yet known, but it seems that contact has been made with an alien life form. One eyewitness says that she saw two aliens come out from a silver ball. They then began to tickle people... TICKLE PEOPLE? Is this some kind of joke? It's not April the First, is it?

The DJ did not believe what he was reading. Katy and I just looked at each other. We knew it was no joke.

Suddenly there was a clattering noise on the radio – as if something had been knocked over. It was followed by another sound, one that we knew already: *heh, heh, heh.* A new note of panic appeared in the DJ's voice.

What's going on? Who's there? Wha—
ladies and gentlemen, this is incredible!
An alien has just made its way into the
studio here at Radio Wow FM. I repeat,
there is a creature from another world
here in the studio with me. It's smiling,
it looks friendly. It's moving towards
me now, it's reaching its arms out.
I think it wants to make contact.
I – oo, hey, don't do that! I'm ticklish
– hahaha, no, heeheehee, hooooo –
sssssssssssssssssssss

The radio went dead.

44

You know what this means, don't you?

Katy nodded. Her eyes were wide.

We both looked upwards. The dark sky was filled with shooting stars. They lit up the night like fireworks, and we knew that each one carried a load of aliens ready to tickle whoever they met.

They're not just in Puddlesford. It's a real invasion isn't it? An invasion of the Ticklers.

45

'Wha– what are we going to do?'
I said, 'There's no point going to the next village, they'll be there as well. It's only a matter of time before they get us…'

I could hear my voice rising with fear.

But Katy seemed calm again. She was grinning.

'I've got an idea,' she said. Her eyes shone. Then she spoke a single word.

Stoneface!

46

CHAPTER 8

Katy has a plan

There was no time to ask her what she was talking about. She was pedalling again, but now she was heading back towards Puddlesford, back towards the High Street... back towards the Ticklers.

A Tickler hopped out into our path. I went to its left, Katy went right. Luckily the Tickler couldn't make up its mind which of us to go for.

47

It waved its arms around trying to decide, and we both rushed past it.

Heh, heh, heh.

It seemed like there were more Ticklers than ever. Another popped out from behind a hedge and made a grab for me. It just caught the edge of my coat, but it didn't get a firm enough grip.

We rode for all we were worth, swerving and dodging and throwing our bikes into almost impossible turns. At last we made it to the other side of the village.

Where are we going?

Back to the school. Don't worry— you'll see why!

We pedalled the rest of the way in silence. Above us, shooting stars were still criss-crossing the skies.

At last we reached the school. All was quiet. The gates were still open, and a single light was on inside the building. It was Mr Watkins' office – Stoneface often worked late at the school in the evening.

We stood very still and listened. We couldn't hear any sounds of laughter. Slowly we stepped into the school grounds.

CHAPTER 9

Stoneface Watkins

It felt strange creeping through the darkened corridors of our school. I knew it all so well.

There was the artwork on the walls, the chairs stacked up on tables, and the bookshelves in the classroom where I sat every day. They all seemed very important to me now. Maybe you change your mind about things when your planet is invaded by tickling aliens?

51

As we went on, I could hear something from further down the corridor. It wasn't laughter and it wasn't the chuckle of the Ticklers. It was someone talking.

Katy had heard it too.

'It's coming from Mr Watkins' office,' she whispered.

We crept closer to the office. Katy slowly pushed the door open and we peeked inside.

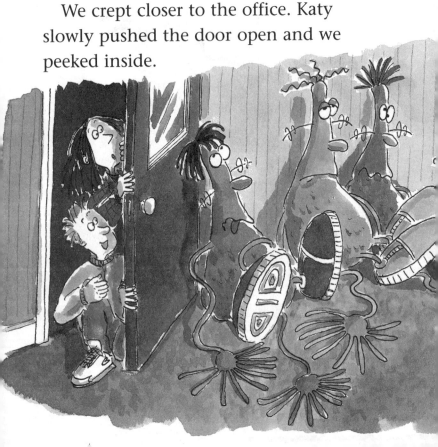

Stoneface Watkins was sitting behind his desk, as usual. He was talking to three Ticklers, but they were not like the ones we had seen before. These Ticklers were slumped against the wall. Their arms hung lifelessly by their sides. Their eyes were glassy, as if they were half-asleep.

'And another thing... I think it is
extremely bad manners to arrive here
without telling us first. It's no excuse to
say that you come from another planet
– good manners are important
anywhere. And as for going around
tickling people! Well, it just isn't on, is
it? You'll have to pull your socks up if
you want to get ahead on Planet Earth.
And another thing...'

Stoneface Watkins went on and on. It was clear what had happened. The Ticklers had attacked, but they had been unable to make the Headteacher laugh. (This wasn't surprising – *nothing* made our Head laugh.) So Stoneface had started to tell them off, and it had sent them all into a kind of sleep-state.

Katy beamed at me.

I knew they'd never get him. Not Stoneface – he's our secret weapon!

I was still worried. I knew it wasn't over yet, not by a long way.

What about all the other Ticklers?

But Katy had thought of this too.

'We'll go with Mr Watkins in his car to the local radio station,' she said. 'We'll break through the Ticklers if we have to. With Stoneface to help us we'll be okay. Then we'll broadcast his voice right across the area. That should do the trick! It'll send them all off to sleep.'

I grinned at Katy.

You're a genius, Katy Skinner!

And that's when it happened. Stoneface Watkins did not stop talking for a moment, but he looked up at us, gave us a little smile... and then he winked at us. Winked! Stoneface Watkins! Sometimes, out of all the amazing things that happened that day, I think that wink was the most amazing thing of all!

The universe is a big place

The plan worked.

Of course it made it into all the newspapers:

Daily Telegram

Headteacher defeats aliens

Gregory Watkins, Headteacher of Puddlesford Junior School, was hailed as a hero yesterday, when he helped put an end to an alien invasion. The alien creatures, known to some as 'Ticklers', had invaded a small area of the country, but it is thought that this was just the beginning of their plans.

Mr Watkins' voice was broadcast from local radio station Radio Wow FM, and it sent many of the aliens into a sleep-like trance, allowing many people to escape.

When questioned by our reporter, Mr Watkins said that he had simply treated the invaders in the same way as he would treat his own pupils.

MR GREGORY WATKINS

Daily Moon

On yer bikes, Ticklers!

The invading army of alien Ticklers got back into their little silver ships yesterday and went back to wherever they come from. An eyewitness who saw one of the ships leave said: 'The creatures seemed keen to go, and they weren't laughing much when they went.'

Inside today's Magic Moon: Ten things you didn't know about those terrible Ticklers – see page 2!

It seemed like every TV programme for a month was about the Ticklers. Of course, nobody could talk about anything else for a while. It isn't every day that aliens try to invade Earth, is it?

But in the end, things went back to normal.

61

School is the same as ever – Mr Watkins' assemblies are still pretty boring, but I don't giggle during them any more. Whenever I feel like giggling, I just remember the way he winked at us that time in his office.

As for me and Katy... we didn't go near Overton's farm for ages. But then one night it just seemed like the right time. We rode up the path near where the Ticklers had landed.

We stopped our bikes at the top of the hill and looked up at the sky. It was a clear night, and we could see lots of stars. I knew Katy was thinking about that night – the night of the Ticklers.

62

It's all over isn't it?

But Katy shook her head uncertainly. She's more serious now than she used to be.

'The universe is a big place, Mike,' she said. 'It must be full of many different life-forms. And now they know that we're here on Earth. And they know we're ticklish...'

About the author

When I was growing up in Manchester, I always wanted to be an astronaut, a footballer, or (if those didn't work out for any reason) perhaps a rock star. So it came as something of a shock when I became first a teacher and then an editor of educational books.

I have lived in Cambridge, Aylesbury, Oxford and Istanbul. I'm still on the run and now live in Chicago with my wife and family. Like Mike in the story, I have read lots of books about alien invasions, so if one ever happens, I think I'm ready!